DATE DUE

Ruby's Wish

To Graeme, for loving my stories—S. Y. B.

To my daughter, Olive, and my dear friend Imogen—S. B.

Text © 2002 by Shirin Yim Bridges.

Illustrations © 2002 by Sophie Blackall.

All rights reserved.

Book design by Kristen M. Nobles.

Typeset in Hiroshige and Ruling Script.

Chinese calligraphy by Jianwei Fong.

The illustrations in this book were rendered in gouache on Arches hot-pressed paper.

Manufactured in Hong Kong.

Library of Congress Cataloging-in-Publication Data

Bridges, Shirin Yim.

Ruby's wish / Shirin Yim Bridges ; [illustrated by] Sophie Blackall.

p. cm.

Summary: In China, at a time when few girls are taught to read or write,

Ruby dreams of going to university with her brothers and male cousins.

ISBN 0-8118-3490-5

[1. Sex role-Fiction. 2. Education-Fiction. 3. China-History—19th century-Fiction.]

I. Blackall, Sophie, ill. II. Title.

PZ7.B75234 Ru 2002

[Fic]—dc21

2001007406

Distributed in Canada by Raincoast Books

9050 Shaughnessy Street, Vancouver, British Columbia V6P 6E5

10 9 8 7 6 5 4

Chronicle Books LLC

85 Second Street, San Francisco, California 94105

www.chroniclekids.com

Ruby's Wish

by Shirin Yim Bridges   illustrated by Sophie Blackall

chronicle books · san francisco

If you walk down a certain road in a
certain city in China, past the pet market
with its yellow-and-green ricebirds hopping in their
bamboo cages, and the goldfish and the terrapins in their
porcelain bowls, you will come to a block of houses, five
houses wide and seven houses deep. Many families live
here now, and the buildings are brown with age and dirt.
But if you look closely, you will see that, once upon a time,
this was all one house, the magnificent home of one family.

The house was built by an old man who returned from the Gold Mountain. That was what the Chinese called California, when many men left to join the Gold Rush there and few came back again. But as I said, this man did come back, and he came back very rich. And he did what rich men did in old China: he married many wives. His wives had many sons, and these sons also had many wives. So at one time, the house was filled with the shrieks and laughter of over one hundred children.

Amongst these children was a little girl that everyone called Ruby, because she loved the color red. In China, red is the color of celebration. On New Year's Day, children receive red envelopes full of good-luck money. Brides wear red on their wedding days. But Ruby insisted on wearing red *every* day. Even when her mother made her wear somber colors like all her other cousins, Ruby would tie up her jet-black hair with red ribbons.

Because he had so many grandchildren, Ruby's grandfather hired a teacher to come to the house. Any grandchild who wanted to learn could join the classes. This was unusual in China in those days, when most girls were never taught to read or write.

Whenever the weather was fine, classes were held in the garden. The windows of Ruby's grandfather's office opened onto that garden. Often, he would rise from his desk to gaze out of his windows at his grandchildren.

One day, Ruby's grandfather looked down from his window to see the high white wall of the garden plastered with calligraphy. His grandchildren had been practicing their handwriting. Ruby's grandfather laughed to see that many had smudged ink on their hands and faces!

Then he noticed a sheet that was more beautiful than
the rest. Which of his grandchildren had produced such
wonderful calligraphy? Down in the garden, the teacher
was praising Ruby. Her ears were turning as bright red
as her jacket.

But if Ruby was doing as well as her boy cousins in her studies, she had to work much harder. When the boys had finished their studies for the day, they were free to play. But the girls had to learn about cooking and keeping house. In fact, as far as their mothers were concerned, these were the *only* things girls had to learn.

One by one, the girls stopped going to the classes. All except Ruby. She would catch up on her embroidery at night. Many nights, her candle flickered long after everyone else had gone to bed.

很不幸生為女子
更不幸生於只疼愛男孩子的這個家庭

One day, the children were asked
to write a poem. Ruby wrote:

*Alas, bad luck to be born a girl; worse luck to be
born into this house where only boys are cared for.*

Ruby's teacher was very impressed by the poem. He
showed it to Ruby's grandfather. Ruby's grandfather
was also impressed, but he was worried about what
the poem said. He summoned Ruby to his office.

Ruby found her grandfather sitting in his chair, her poem spread open on his desk.

"Did you write this poem?" asked Ruby's grandfather.

"Yes I did, Grandfather," answered Ruby.

"Do you really think that in this house we only care for boys?"

"Oh no, Grandfather," said Ruby, very sorry that she had upset him. "You take good care of all of us, and for that we are all grateful."

"Little Ruby," her grandfather said gently, "I really would like to know why you wrote this poem. How are the boys better looked after?"

"Well," said Ruby, trying to think of a small, unimportant thing, "when it is the Moon Festival and we are each given half a moon cake, the boys always get the half with the yellow moon yolk."

"Hmmm," said her grandfather, as if he was still waiting. "Is that so?"

"Yes," continued Ruby, "and when it is the Lantern Festival, the girls are given simple paper lanterns but the boys have red lanterns in the shapes of goldfish, cockerels and dragons."

Ruby's grandfather chuckled. He'd never thought about it before. He could imagine how much Ruby would have liked a red lantern.

"But most importantly," said Ruby, staring hard at her red shoes, "the boys will get to go to university, but the girls will be married."

"Don't you want to be married?" asked her grandfather. "You know, you are very lucky. A daughter of this house can marry any man."

"I know, Grandfather," said Ruby, "but I'd much rather go to university."

Ruby's grandfather touched her hair. "Thank you for talking to me, Ruby," he said. "Go on with your lessons. Make the most of them while you can."

So Ruby went on with her lessons. Some of the boys grew up and went away to university. Some stayed in the house and started families of their own. But when they grew up, all the girls were married and sent away to live in their husbands' homes. Ruby knew it would soon be her turn. In the ponds, Ruby could see the orange-and-white carp gulping for breath under a thin layer of ice. It would soon be Chinese New Year. Ruby felt sure it would be her last one at home.

On New Year's Day, Ruby put on red velvet shoes
and tied red ribbons in her hair. Then she went to
wish everyone a happy new year. She started with her
married cousins, then worked her way up through her
parents, aunts and uncles. Each one gave her a red
packet full of lucky money. Finally, she bowed before
her grandfather. "Good luck and prosperity, Grandfather,"
she said.

"Good luck, little Ruby," replied her grandfather, and he
handed her a very fat red packet.

Ruby could feel the eyes of all her family on her as she
opened the lucky red envelope. Can you guess what was
in it? It wasn't money, it was something much better
than that.

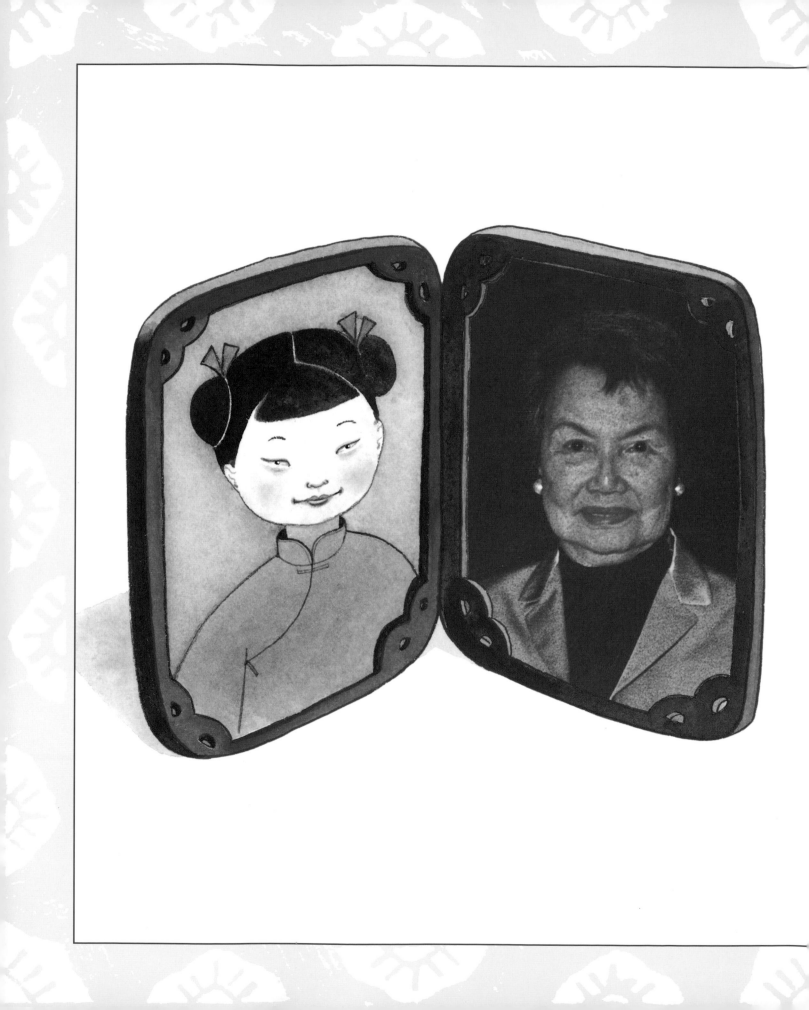

It was a letter from a university, saying that they would be proud to accept Ruby as one of their very first female students.

So that's how Ruby got her wish. It's a true story. And how do I know this? Well, Ruby is my grandmother, and every day she still wears a little red.